Clive Eats Alligators

Alison Lester

For Will and Clair

SCHOLASTIC INC.

New York   Toronto   London   Auckland   Sydney

Breakfast

Frank eats granola.

Celeste has tea and toast in bed.

Nicky has a banana.

Rosie likes eggs and bacon.

Tessa eats a sausage.

Ernie has porridge.

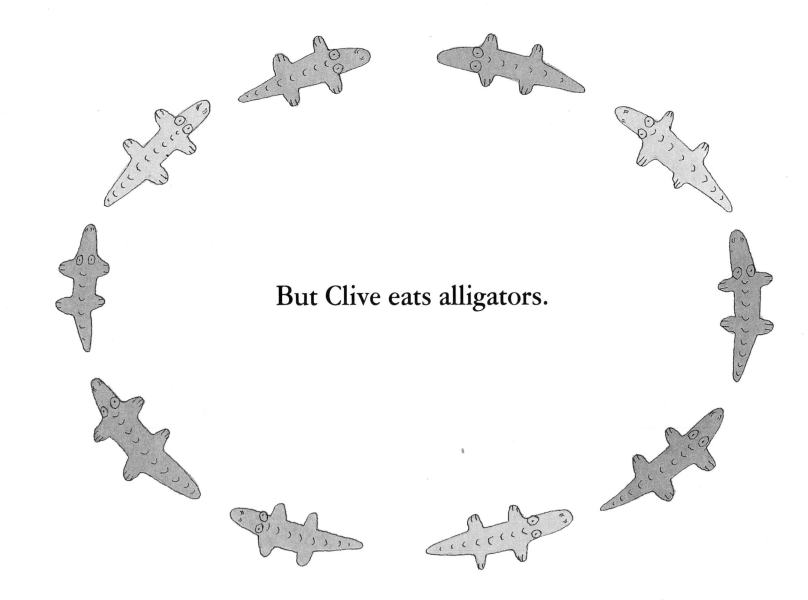

But Clive eats alligators.

Getting dressed

Rosie wears a cowboy hat.

Frank has stripey trousers.

Nicky likes her overalls.

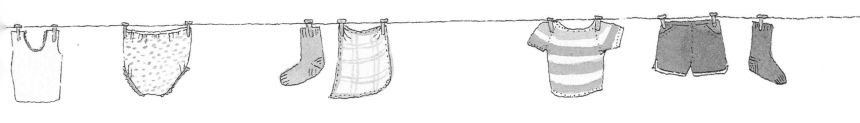

Ernie wears a
dog-and-cat
pullover.

Celeste wears a
tutu.

Clive wears an
alligator T-shirt.

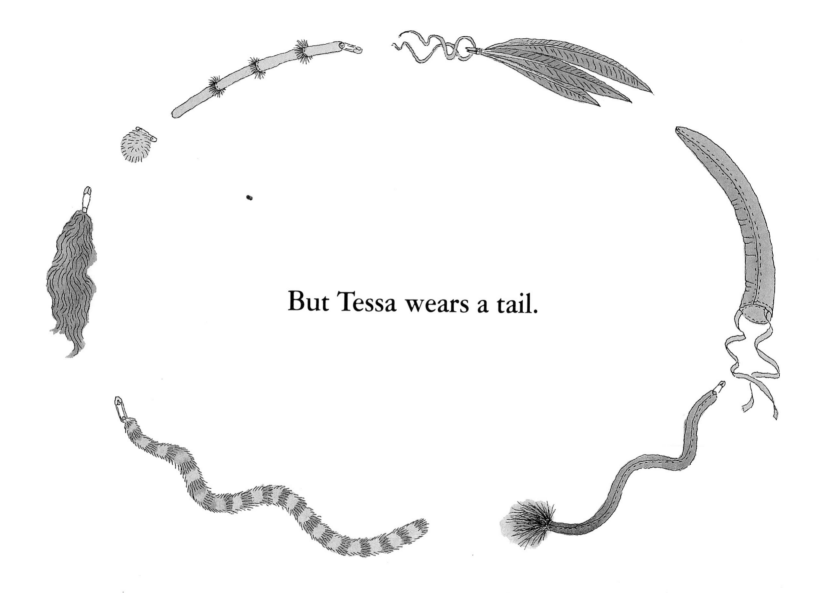

But Tessa wears a tail.

Playing

Clive is painting.

Celeste is dressing up.

Ernie makes a dinosaur.

Nicky builds a
tree house.

Rosie's on the
swing.

Tessa's in the
sandbox.

But Frank plays chess with Roger.

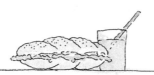 # Lunch

Celeste has a picnic.

Tessa has a
tea party.

Clive eats at his
favorite café.

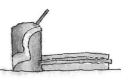

Ernie has
sandwiches down
on the pier.

Frank has a snack
on his bed.

Rosie has a hamburger
in the truck.

But Nicky has lunch in her tree house.

Shopping

Celeste visits the
pet shop.

Frank likes the
bookshop.

Tessa goes to the
butcher shop.

Nicky likes the
hardware shop.

Clive visits the
toy shop.

Rosie likes the
sweet shop.

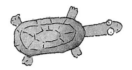

But Ernie loves to visit the animal museum.

NOT FOR SALE

Pets

Tessa has a calico
cat.

Clive has two
goldfish.

Frank loves his dog.

Nicky has a
guinea pig.

Rosie has a pony.

Ernie has a tortoise.

But Celeste loves her rooster.

Treats

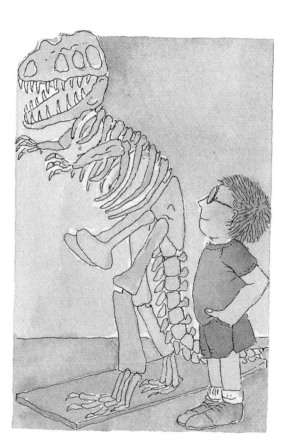

Nicky loves the beach.

Ernie likes to go to the museum.

Celeste enjoys the ballet.

Frank likes
holidays.

Tessa loves her
birthday.

Clive goes to the
zoo.

But Rosie loves the rodeo.

Bedtime

Frank has his blue blanket.

Ernie leaves his night light on.

Tessa takes her teddy bear.

Nicky hugs her rag
doll.

Celeste listens to
her music box.

Rosie likes the top
bunk.

But . . .
what do you think Clive does?